Beauty and the Beast

Illustrated by Victor Tavares

Retold by Louie Stowell
Designed by Samantha Meredith

Once upon a foggy day,
a merchant was riding home.

Suddenly, a whispering wind blew the fog away,

and he saw a mysterious
castle looming up ahead.

The castle gates creaked open.
The merchant rode inside and called, "Hello!"

But no one answered.

In the castle hall he found a table, laid with a feast.
To his surprise, a plate floated to him through the air.

"An enchanted castle!" thought the merchant.
He was unable to resist the hot, delicious food.

Then he
wandered into
the castle gardens.

Beauty *loves* roses!

The merchant picked a flower
to give to his daughter, Beauty.

There was a deafening roar. "You thief!"
growled a hideous creature, springing from the bushes.

You stole my rose!
Now you must die!

"P... p... please don't kill me!" begged the merchant.
"The rose isn't for me, it's for my daughter."

Then bring her to me. If she refuses you must return to meet your fate!

The merchant
rode slowly home.

He told Beauty about the
castle and the terrible Beast.

"I'll have to go back," he said.
"I won't put you in danger!"

But Beauty wasn't afraid.
She waited until her
father was in his study...

...then galloped
to the Beast's castle.

As soon as the Beast saw Beauty, he fell in love.

"Please stay with me,"
he begged. He looked so
lonely that Beauty agreed.

"I'll stay for
a while, at least,"
she promised.

That night, the Beast told Beauty a magical tale.

"You seem so human
when you talk," she said.

After dinner, the Beast went down on one knee.
"Marry me, Beauty!" he cried. "I love you!"

"I'm sorry, Beast, but I don't love you," she replied.

He nodded sadly
and said goodnight.

The next day, Beauty
explored the castle.

She wandered down echoing
corridors, through the vast library
and up into towering turrets.

In the evening, the Beast went down on one knee again.
"I love you, Beauty. Please marry me!" he begged.

I'm sorry, I can't.
I don't love you.

The following night, he asked again.
But Beauty's answer was just the same.

As the days passed, Beauty grew sad.
"I miss my father," she told the Beast.

In reply, he handed her a sparkling ring.

"I still won't marry you,"
said Beauty, quickly.

"Oh!" exclaimed the Beast. "I wasn't going to ask
you that. This magic ring will take you home."

"I promise I'll come back soon," said Beauty.

She put on the ring and vanished in a swirl of glittering smoke.

Seconds later, she was home.

She stayed with her father for a week,
but every day she missed the Beast.

Until one night she had an awful dream...

The beast is dying!
I have to go to him!

The ring carried Beauty back to the Beast's castle.

She called out, "Beast!
Beast!
Where are you?"

Beauty ran into the garden.
The Beast lay, barely breathing, on the ground.

"Please don't die, Beast," Beauty cried.

"I love you!"

You came back...

As she spoke to him
there was a blinding flash
and a deafening bang!

The Beast disappeared.

In his place there was a handsome prince.

"Beast?" asked Beauty. "Is that you? What happened?"

"A wicked, jealous fairy cursed me long ago..." the prince explained.

"...but your love broke the spell!"

Beauty and the prince
were married the next day.

I hope they're
miserable!

And they lived...

...happily ever after!

Curses!

Edited by Jenny Tyler, Susanna Davidson and Lesley Sims.
Digital manipulation by Will Dawes.